STORYTELLERS: ADVENTURES IN THE STORYBOOK EMPIRE

**Written By
Brian K. Wagner**

Illustrated By Kat Boykott

Copyright © 2018 Animated Brand Media

All rights reserved.

Dedicated To
Lisa and the real Bennett

Bennett is an explorer who travels from countryside to countryside and village to village telling his stories. He brings color and joy to all that hear the stories he has to tell. Walking is how he travels to where he is going, and Bennett walks everywhere he goes. He has walked…

…Not hundreds of steps, Not hundreds of thousands of steps, but hundreds of millions of steps.

The more Bennett travels, the more adventures he gathers and the more people he meets to tell his stories. You see, traveling is how people discover new stories; they are created by seeing and doing.

One warm sunny day, the explorer was walking in South America at its southern most tip, in the foothills of the Andes Mountains, when he suddenly turned east towards Chile and announced to himself, "Today I'm going to discover something new."

While crossing a shallow river, Bennett approached a vast, dark and steamy rainforest.

Though the sun lit up the outside of the rainforest beautifully, the trail leading into it was so dark it looked like he was about to enter a cave. Vines and low growing trees were all around. Bennett had never seen anything like this before; he knew he needed to be brave. He ventured into the trees and with each step he took it got darker and darker.

As he emerged, he realized his journeys had never taken him anywhere like what now appeared. Building after building rose before him, an entire city made from BOOKs…

...Not hundreds of books, Not hundreds of thousands of books but hundreds of millions of books.

From the tallest of tall to the smallest of small, everything was constructed out of stacks and stacks of books. Unlike the rainforest surrounding it, the city's buildings were gray and colorless.

All the citizens seemed unhappy as they went about their day.

Amazed and curious, Bennett entered the city and peeked through one of the books. He couldn't believe his eyes; the pages were all EMPTY! He looked in several other books but there wasn't a word anywhere.

"I wonder what would happen if I wrote down one of my stories? Maybe that would bring a little color to the people that live here," Bennett thought to himself.

He opened a small book that he pulled from a part of the wall and began to write about magic, mystery and friendship. As he wrote, the wall began to change color! It became a cheerful blue, red and then green. When he finished the wall had been transformed with beautiful colorful designs.

A crowd of citizens had started to gather while Bennett was writing. One of them bravely stepped forward to the new visitor and said. "Thank you, young traveler, for sharing this gift with us. You must come and meet King Bemis. He will be most interested in your talents."

Up the hill walked the explorer to the King's castle. The castle was very gloomy, as well as its towers were dreary. Even the knights guarding the castle looked miserable, their armor stained and tarnished.

The King was so pleased to meet Bennett and after welcoming him, he began telling his own story of his kingdom.

Once upon a time there was a Wise King that had a son, a young prince. One day the King told the prince to go out into the country, past the great mountains and into the rainforest and find his treasure. The following day that is exactly what the young prince did.

Everywhere he traveled, the prince walked. He went to many lands and kingdoms and was well liked by the countless people he met.

One day on his travels he ventured into the rainforest in the southern most tip of Chile and came upon the ruins of a great empire. He looked all around but all he could find were books. Mountains of stacked books were everywhere and all the pages of the books were EMPTY.

Since there was so many books scattered around, the young prince decided to use the books to build a place where people could live and be happy. It was a land like no one had ever seen before.

Travelers discovered the kingdom made from books and they all loved the kind young prince so much that they deemed him King Bemis, the Kind King. Even though all the citizens loved the King and were happy in their new home, there was still something missing. The King knew it too and promised one day all that would change.

"Could you help me keep my promise?" the King said to Bennett after telling his story.

Bennett was so moved by the King's request that he told the King he would continue writing his stories throughout the kingdom and bring color and joy everywhere. He would start with the castle.

When all the stories were written into the books of the King's castle it was the grandest palace anyone had ever seen; it gleamed like a jewel. Giant books of dragons and knights made up parts of the sidewalls of the castle. Storybooks about princesses covered the roof. Tales of pirates and ocean journeys made up the rampart and drawbridge. Books with golden colored spines supported the towers where the Kind King himself stayed.

The Knights that guarded the castle were now bright and proud, their armor shining like mirrors in the sun.

This new empire became so beautiful and colorful that it created a rainbow that rose all the way into the sky past the highest of the kingdom's tallest building.

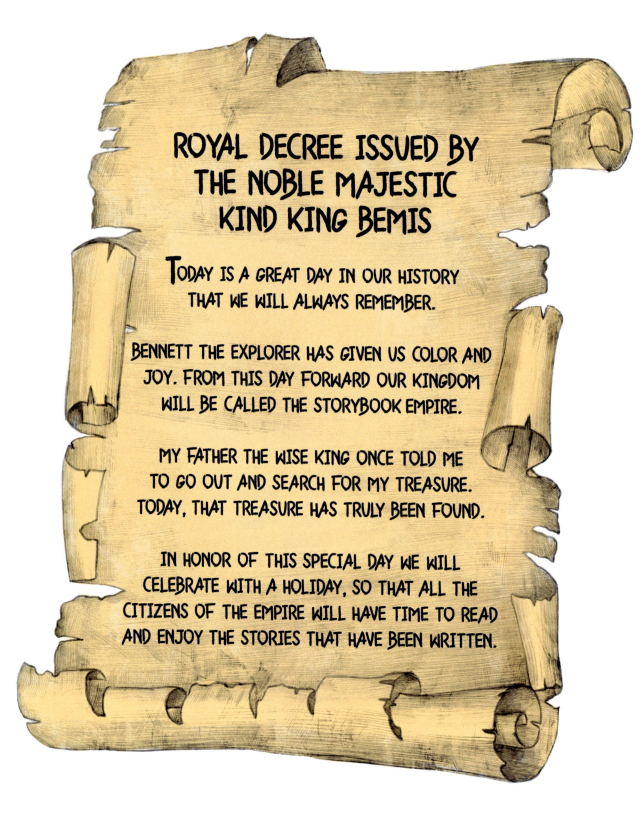

Royal Decree Issued By The Noble Majestic Kind King Bemis

Today is a great day in our history that we will always remember.

Bennett the explorer has given us color and joy. From this day forward our kingdom will be called the Storybook Empire.

My father the wise king once told me to go out and search for my treasure. Today, that treasure has truly been found.

In honor of this special day we will celebrate with a holiday, so that all the citizens of the empire will have time to read and enjoy the stories that have been written.

The citizens of the empire were so pleased with what Bennett did for their kingdom that they all joined together and wrote a book. This book was about a certain Storytelling Explorer that told…

…Not hundreds of stories, Not hundreds of thousands of stories but hundreds of millions of stories.

Made in the USA
Columbia, SC
22 October 2018